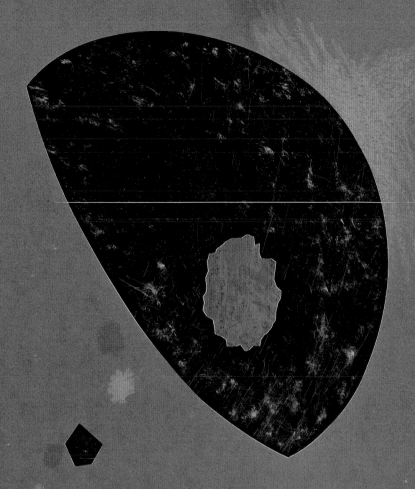

Copyright © 1998 by Nord-Süd Verlag AG, Gossau Zürich, Switzerland
First published in Switzerland under the title Wo der Mond wohnt.
English translation copyright © 1998 by North-South Books Inc.

First published in the United States, Great Britain, Canada,
Australia, and New Zealand in 1998 by North-South Books,
an imprint of Nord-Süd Verlag AG, Gossau Zürich, Switzerland.

Distributed in the United States by North-South Books Inc., New York.

Library of Congress Cataloging-in-Publication Data is available.
A CIP catalogue record for this book is available from The British Library.
ISBN 1-55858-921-X (trade binding)
10 9 8 7 6 5 4 3 2 1

Printed in Belgium

IVAN GANTSCHEV WHERE
THE MOON LIVES

TRANSLATED BY ANDREW CLEMENTS

A MICHAEL NEUGEBAUER BOOK
NORTH-SOUTH BOOKS / NEW YORK / LONDON

An old farmhouse sat beside a lake.

ndow, Father Duck made
cement one day.

"There are sounds coming from

It was true.
First came little quacking sounds...

and then a baby duckling burst out of the egg
and into the sunshine!

The world was so large, and the duckling was so small.

He had a lot to learn—so he asked his father a lot of questions.

"Why is the sun so close to the ground?
Is water always wet?
How many rocks make a mountain?"

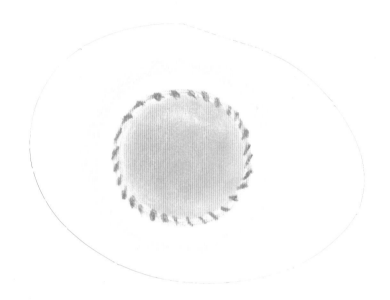

Each day the duckling discovered something new,
and each day he had more questions.
"Why is the sun so high above us now?
Will the sky always be blue?
Does a tree know how to swim?"

But of all the things the duckling discovered,
the most beautiful was the moon.
"Where does the moon live?"
he asked as he watched it rise beyond the lake.

Father Duck didn't know anything about the moon.
"You will have ask the wise old swan," he said.

When the sun went down,
the duckling began to paddle toward the swan's island.
At first the lake was dark and scary. The duckling wanted to
turn back.

But then the moon rose into the sky, shining clear and bright.
The duckling smiled and kept on paddling.

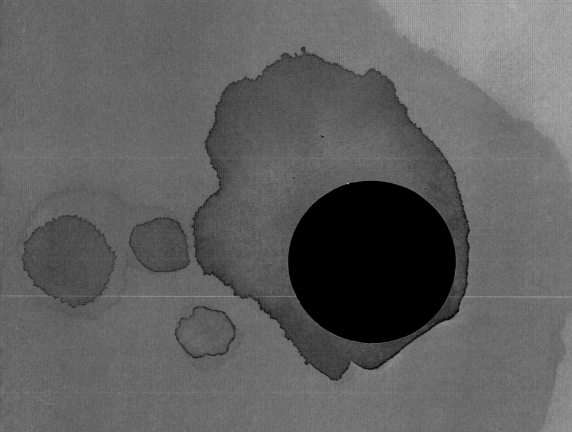

It was a long, long way to the island.

The duckling was getting tired,
but the island was getting closer—
and the moon looked bigger and bigger.
It was so beautiful.

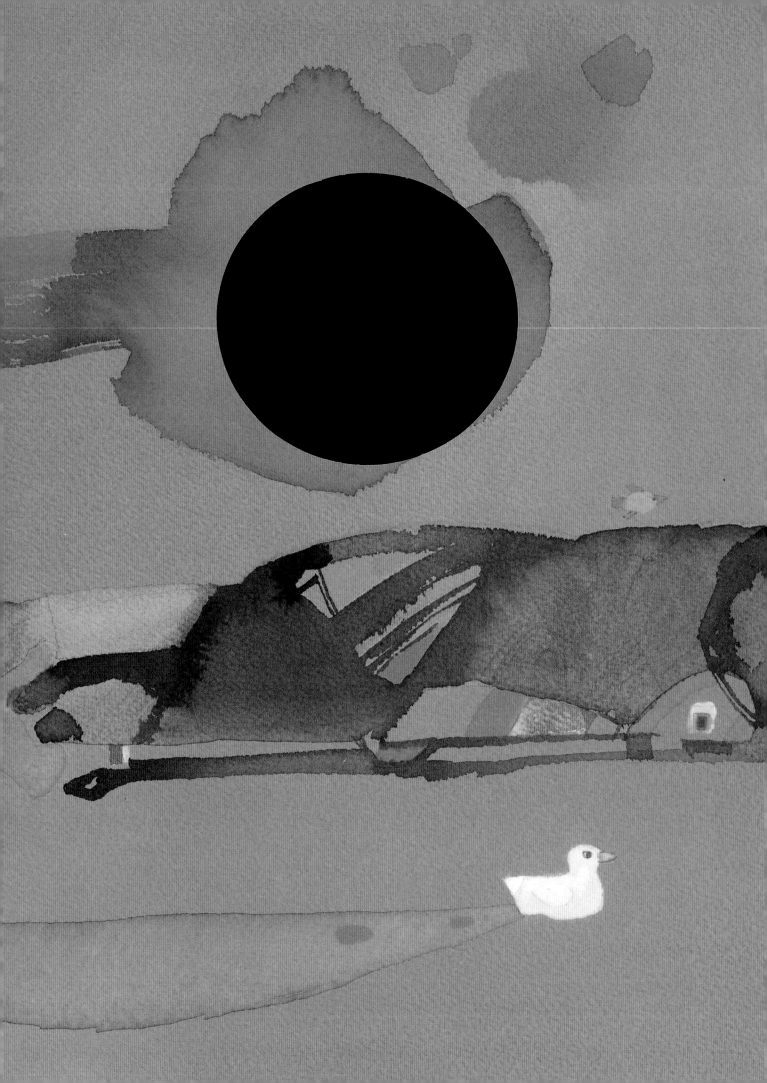

The duckling kept swimming, and now the moon looked very big.
It began to disappear behind the island, right behind the swan's house.

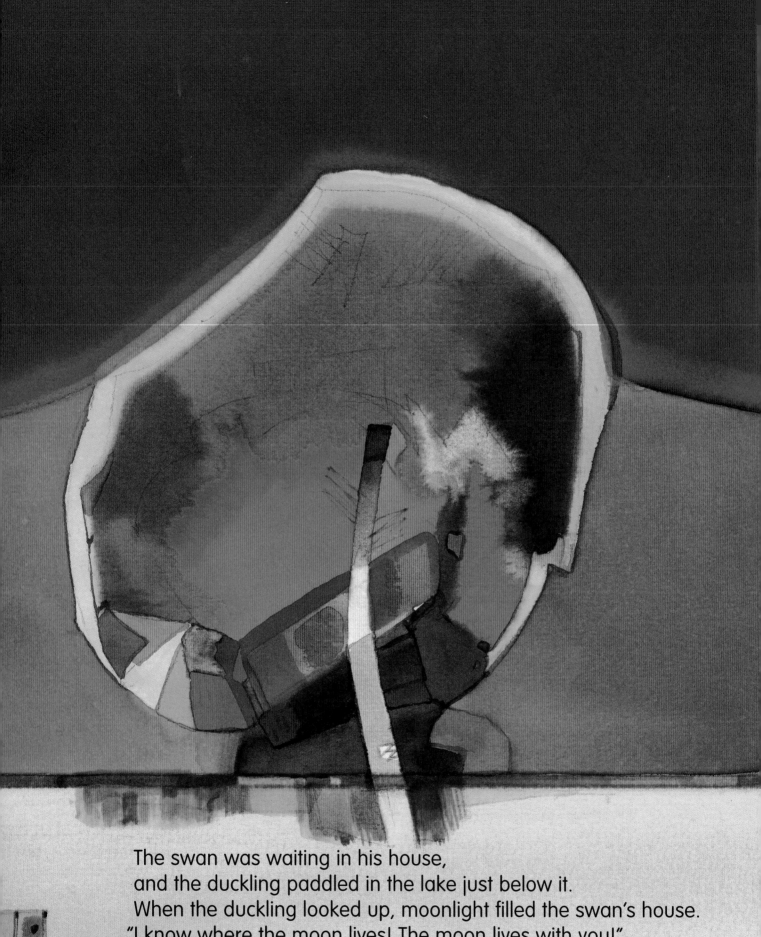

The swan was waiting in his house,
and the duckling paddled in the lake just below it.
When the duckling looked up, moonlight filled the swan's house.
"I know where the moon lives! The moon lives with you!"

The swan chuckled.
"It may look that way, little duck, but it isn't so.
The moon lives in all the sky, above and around
the earth.
Night after night, year after year,
around and around the earth goes the moon.
When you see the moon go down, for someone else,
it is rising!"

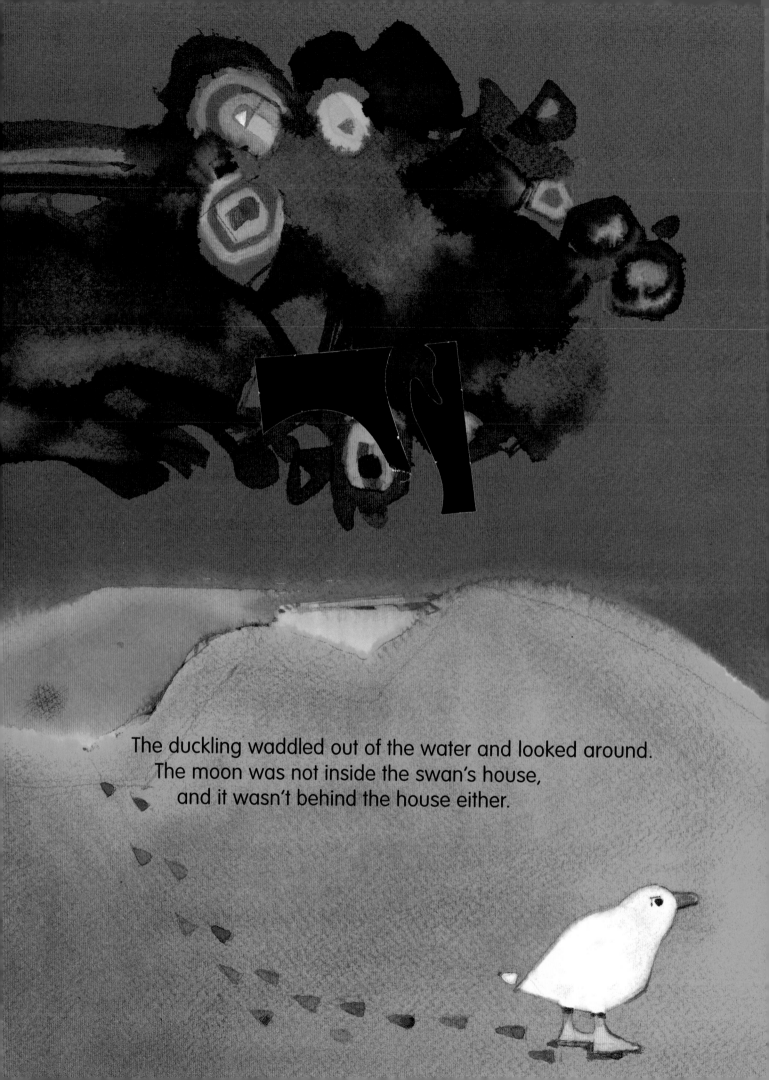

The duckling waddled out of the water and looked around.
The moon was not inside the swan's house,
and it wasn't behind the house either.

Then the duckling saw the moon hanging in the sky above the lake.
The moon was lovely, perfect.
Slowly, slowly, it sank and disappeared.
And the duckling remembered
what the swan had said:
"When you see the moon go down,
for someone else, it is rising."

In the morning, when the duckling was halfway home,
he saw his father, waiting for him.
"Did you learn where the moon lives?"

The duckling was carrying a swan's feather, pale and
bright as the moon.
"Yes, and I learned the secret of the moon's beauty, too."

Father Duck said, "Secret? What secret?"

The duckling said,
"I learned that the moon lives in all the sky.
It shines on every lake and every mountain and every tree.
And I learned that when <u>we</u> see the moon go down,
for someone else, the moon is rising.
The secret of the moon's beauty is simple:
The moon never stops sharing."

Then the duckling and his father paddled the rest
of the way home together.

ALICIA